D0251562

I CAN READ IT ALL BY MYSELF

Beginner Books

The Berenstain Bears and the Missing DINOSAUR BONE

BEGINNER BOOKS
A Division of Random House, Inc.

The Berenstain Bears and the Missing DINOSAUR

Stan and Jan Berenstain

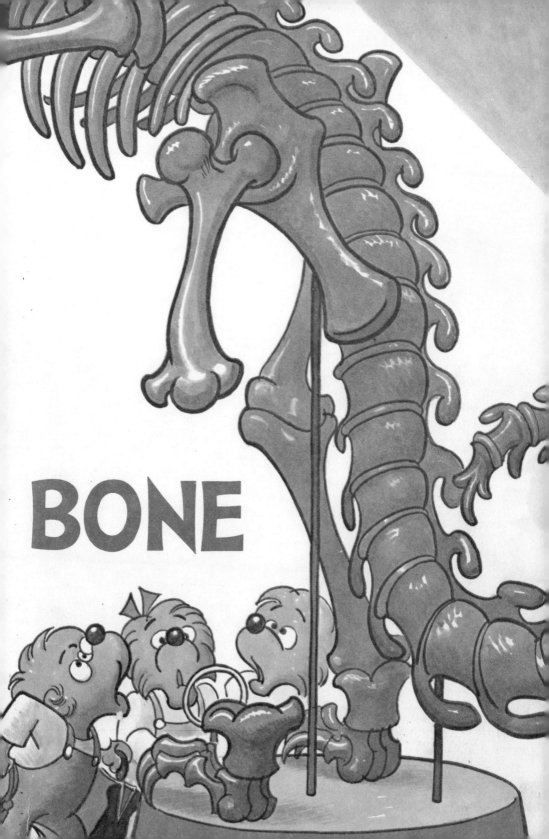

Library of Congress Cataloging in Publication Data
Berenstain, Stanley. The Berenstain Bears and the missing dinosaur bone. SUMMARY: The three Bear Detectives search for a dinosaur bone that is missing from the Bear Museum. [1. Mystery and detective stories. 2. Bears—Fiction. 3. Stories in rhyme] I. Berenstain, Jan joint author. II. Title PZ8.3.B4493Bg [E] 79-3458 ISBN 0-394-84447-5 ISBN 0-394-94447-X (lib. bdg.)

Manufactured in the United States of America

Bears lining up

outside the door.

Dr. Bear, inside,

pacing the floor.

What's wrong in there?
What's up? What's up?
wonder three little bears
and one little pup.

A dinosaur bone
is missing in there!
"Somebody took it!"
said Dr. Bear.
"Who took that bone?
Who took it? Where?"

Three little bears
and their hound dog, Snuff,
come inside
with their detective stuff.

There's no case too hard,
no case too tough,
for the Bear Detectives
and their hound dog, Snuff!

The search begins!
And none too soon.
The Bear Museum
opens at noon.

They will search the place.

Every cranny and nook.

Will they find the bone?

Will they find the crook?

A dark, dark room.

A mummy's tomb!

Is that the thief?
That spooky face?

No.

That's the museum's

mummy case.

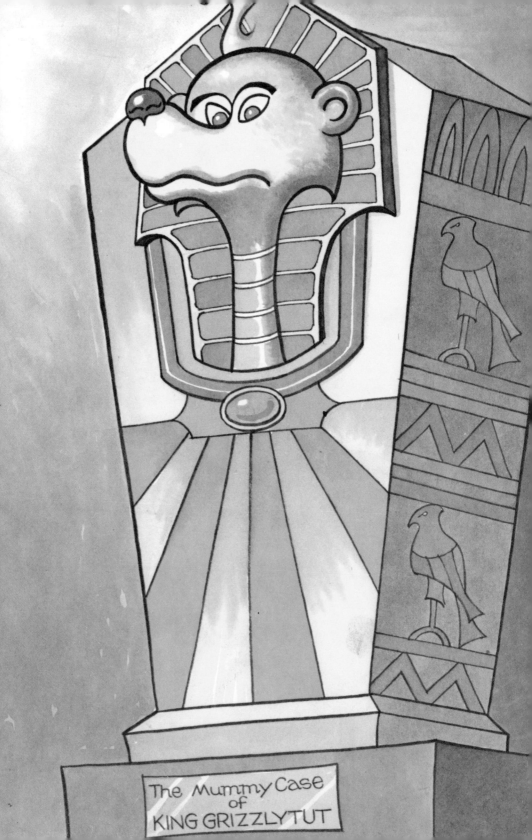

The Mummy Case
of
KING GRIZZLYTUT

Eleven fifteen.

Time grows short.

Now, where would one hide

a bone of that sort?

It could be there,
inside that vase.
The bone thief's
perfect hiding place!

VALUABLE
VASE

"You can look
in that valuable vase
if you must.
There's nothing
in there
but some valuable dust."

Not much time left.
Just half an hour!
The Bear Detectives
search the tower.

Wrong again.
That's an
Indian totem pole.

It's getting late
but still they look.
And still no bone,
and still no crook.

"Say . . .

maybe bone thieves work in packs.

Three thieves!

With a sword, and a gun, and an ax!"

Wrong again!
It's the museum's
famous statues of wax!

They had better find
that leg bone soon.
There's just one minute
left till noon!

With no more time
to search and look,
they know they will not
catch that crook.

They failed!
This case is much too hard. . . .

Wait! . . .

What's that out there
in the yard?

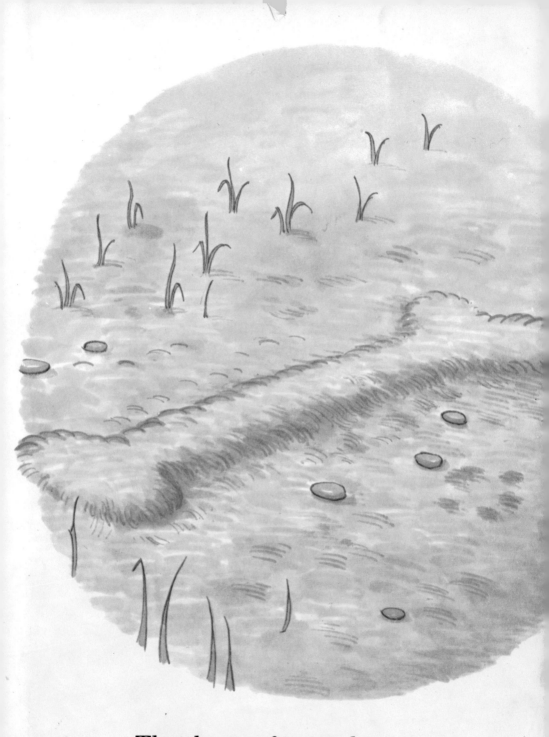

That lump of ground—
that bone-shaped mound!

The missing bone!

It's found! It's found!

With hound dog paw prints
all around.

THE CASE IS SOLVED!

No job's too hard,
no case too tough,
for the Bear Detectives . . .

and that

bone thief, Snuff.

Stan and Jan Berenstain

Several years ago Stan and Jan Berenstain were captured by a family of bears. The funny, furry group came out of the woods behind their studio in Bucks County, Pennsylvania, and cavorted  about on their drawing boards with the other cartoon folk already in residence there. While the foibles of the Berenstain people had been enjoyed by millions of grown-ups in books and magazines, the wacky adventures of the Berenstain Bears soon became favorites of millions of young readers around the world.

The Berenstains' two sons have outgrown bears—one is a scientist who works with and writes about monkeys and the other is an artist who writes and illustrates books about children's many other favorite things, from castles to trolls.